Mommy's Hands

KATHRYN LASKY & JANE KAMINE   Pictures by DARCIA LaBROSSE

HYPERION BOOKS FOR CHILDREN

New York

I love my mommy's hands.
I love the way my little hand fits into
her big hand when we walk.
She says, "Your hand is as warm as a biscuit."

Mommy loves the way my hands pull her face close when we talk.

And I say, "I can count your freckles."

I love to watch my
mommy's hands pour
cereal into a bowl and
then the milk.
Her hands never
spill a drop.

And Mommy loves the way I can snap the snaps
on my snowsuit now with no help.

Even though my hair is short,
my mommy's hands can braid it—
one teeny-weeny braid
that stands straight up.
I say, "Wow! I love it."

Mommy likes the way my hands dribble wet sand for
decoration on the sand castle we build at the beach.
She says, "Wow, what pretty dribbles!"

Sometimes our hands do things together.
When we mix cookie dough we don't use spoons,
and our hands get all tangled up in the bowl.

Mommy fits her hands over mine on the rolling pin to roll out the dough.

Then we cut out our favorite shapes to eat together later.

In the winter our hands make frost pictures
on the cold windowpanes.

In the spring we dig holes for radishes and carrots
and pansies and Johnny-jump-ups.

My hands pick the flowers and pull the
vegetables out of the ground.
Mommy's hands slice the carrots and the
radishes for snacks.

On summer nights I like the way Mommy's
hands point at the shooting stars.
Her hands trace starry pictures in the sky—the Big Bear,
the Little Dipper, the Swan, the Archer, the Eagle.

Sometimes Mommy helps me write my name. I hold the pencil, and Mommy's hand holds mine, and we make the letters together.

Mommy's hands make hard things easy.
I like to watch her fingers pick out knots from my shoelaces.

Mommy's hands zip off Band-Aids so fast.
We both shout "Ouch!" at the same time.

At bedtime the last thing Mommy's hands
do is tuck me in and smooth the blanket.
And most of all I love her hands when they
touch my face and she kisses me good night.
And I say, "I can still count your freckles,
even in the dark."

For Phoebe, who loves her mom's hands—K.L. & J.K.
For Maman Céline and Petit René—D. L.

Text © 2002 by Kathryn Lasky and Jane Kamine

Illustrations © 2002 by Darcia LaBrosse

For information address Hyperion Books for Children,
114 Fifth Avenue, New York, New York 10011-5690.

First Edition

1 3 5 7 9 10 8 6 4 2

Printed in Mexico

LIBRARY OF CONGRESS CATALOGING-IN-PUBLICATION DATA on file

ISBN 0-7868-0280-4 (hc)

Visit www.hyperionchildrensbooks.com